ALEKSANDR VOINOV
SKYBOUND

RIPTIDE
PUBLISHING

Riptide Publishing
PO Box 6652
Hillsborough, NJ 08844
http://www.riptidepublishing.com

Skybound

Cover Art by Jordan Taylor, www.jordantaylorbooks.com/jt/Cover_Art.html
Editors: JoSelle Vanderhooft and Rachel Haimowitz
Layout: L.C. Chase, www.lcchase.com/design.htm

ISBN: 978-1-937551-82-7

First edition
December, 2012

Also available in ebook.
ISBN: 978-1-937551-49-0

To my padawan, Peter, who gleefully told me what firing an anti-tank weapon feels like.

When he comes down again, his plane is steaming like a war horse. It is cold up there, despite the heat of battle. We all rush to him. Few others' hearts are racing like mine, I expect. Mine is rattling like a badly maintained engine. The harsh tack-tack sound is hollow and sad and more dangerous than empty ammunition boxes in the middle of a dogfight.

The others are landing, too, steel eagles rolling over the tarmac; I don't have time to count them. I'm normally counting the empty spaces. The absences. But I never count them in his *Staffel*. Nobody else exists to me when he lands. Everything stops existing when he takes off, as if he takes it all with him when he goes up there, to places I'll never see again. That vast open non-place of emptiness that becomes significant only when his comrades are there, too, and of course the enemy fighters guarding the bombers bound for Berlin.

I freeze outside the small crowd greeting him as he pushes out of the cockpit—now the only animated part of the steel bird—briefly separating from it to drink, eat, rest while I care for the shell he leaves behind. Even from here I can see this was a bad fight. There's a hole low in the cockpit window, the very end point of a line of them along the nose of the Messerschmitt Bf 109. I don't expect to find a single bullet in the boxes when we open them up, but there might be a bullet meant for the pilot inside the cockpit.

He all but vanishes in the welcoming crowd, which is our signal. Like my other black-clad brethren, I'm there foremost for the plane, to fix what can be fixed, clean up what needs to be cleaned, to reload and refuel.

We push the plane to the side of the tarmac where we *Schwarzen Männer*, the "black men," work, lately in grim silence. We know the bird needs to fly—there are few enough of them as it is, and while we dawdle, Berlin is burning, just as Hamburg has burned. This

Jagdgeschwader is hunting bombers, downing them before they reach the city, if our pilots are lucky.

I used to count the absences when they landed.

There is a lot of work. They fight by day. They fight by night. We repair and reload whenever they come back. Once they receive word that bombers are en route, they jump out of their bunks, rookies and *Experten* alike, and get ready to fight. It's the rookies who don't last very long. At the speed at which the pilots are hurled again and again into the sky, many never make it. Their training is rushed, they are thrown into battle with hardly any flight hours at all, they cannot rest enough, and they take risks because they don't know any better.

The Messerschmitt is not an easy plane. It can be volatile during landing and takeoff. It has pride; it doesn't yield to just any man. Those who subdue it become old hands in a few flights.

It's late at night when I sit near a wing on my toolbox. I can't sleep. The cloud cover I see beyond the open hangar doors is heavy, no moon visible. This might be a flight night, or it might not be, but I'm not holding out much hope. This bird is ready to go. I fitted a new canopy myself—parts aren't easy to come by, but there are wrecks I can salvage. Peter Christensen taught me everything I know about this, before they moved him west for a great offensive and he never came back.

I sit, smoking, my head against the cool comfort of the fighter plane's wheel, its wing shielding but never embracing me. I'm a cold nestling tonight.

I want to read, but the situation won't allow it. The leaden lump of what we're doing and the sheer desperation of it stifles every thought of returning to the thick Karl May book I'd been reading. Adventure stories, where evil always loses in the end, defeated by the German hero and his American blood brother. The very idea feels like sacrilege now—there won't be a red-skinned Indian brave to cover any German's back. No cattle thieves, no bandits fighting over lost treasure in the endless prairie. This here is serious, and as far away as it can be from a schoolboy's dreams.

And those other dreams, too. I must be the only one who felt an odd, deeper thrill at the rites of blood brotherhood in those books, of a friendship as deep as destiny that bound those characters together. Companions of my childhood, whispering words that inspired my sweaty dreams when I was old enough to see a deeper meaning. I would devote myself like this to another man. Take the bullet meant for him, and die in his arms, knowing I had fulfilled my destiny.

But I'm no Indian brave.

Steps circle the plane. I straighten up, expecting I-don't-know-who. An inspection. My former superior, Christensen, who barked at me not to smoke anywhere near the priceless machines, his Berliner accent thick and comical but for his glare and his tendency to grab you by the scruff of your neck if you didn't jump immediately. I never expected I'd miss him, but I guess I do.

I didn't expect *him*, certainly not in uniform, and a recklessly dishevelled one at that. I'm about to jump up when he pushes an empty ammunition box closer to me and simply sits down, waving off any startled movement I could make. I've never spoken to him. Will he speak? Wordlessly, I offer him a cigarette, and he plucks it from the packet.

It's the first time I see his hands, normally wrapped in black leather. His nails are so short that if they were any shorter, they'd bare the quick underneath. They are cut, not bitten.

I rub my hands on my coveralls before I offer him fire; he bends closer to take the flame rather than the lighter. My hands are steady, even though I expect them to lose that at any moment. I've never been so relieved to be able to snap the lighter shut, though I could have watched his face illuminated by fire for an hour. There's a reflection of flame in his features, like in the painting of an old master. Flesh made light. I pull on my own cigarette, watch him cross his uniformed legs, then cross mine, realize what I'm doing and put them firmly back where they were.

"Felix, isn't it?"

I almost swallow my cigarette, then manage to nod, wishing I had some more words, something as remotely as natural and nonchalant as his.

"The lucky one," he continues, before inhaling smoke.

I'm tongue-tied. The idea that I will say something stupid is more mortifying than him thinking me a gaping idiot. "Don't feel so lucky," I choke out.

He looks at me. Dark blue eyes. But the feature I admire most is his forehead, the eyebrows. They look heroic, for want of a better word. My mother reads physiognomy books and says that the curve of the forehead expresses willpower. If it is shaped like a ram's, the person it belongs to will push through a wall. The *Leutnant*'s forehead is that of a conqueror, then. Clear, strong features not out of place in a weekly newsreel.

"Why's that?" he asks patiently, then his face falls and he looks down and to the side for a moment. "I guess it's personal."

Oh God, does he think my family was trapped in a firestorm? I'm on the verge of stuttering, but manage to catch myself. "I wish I could fight, *Herr Leutnant*."

He regards me curiously.

"I dreamt of flying. As a boy, I mean."

One corner of his mouth pulls up. Now he looks more like the fighter ace, the man who makes my hands shake. He must hear that a lot. He's a legend. Every green boy desires to be him. I don't. My desires are more complicated. "And?"

"I did not pass the test," I admit, even though it kills me a little inside. He can laugh at me or mock me. That would make all of this easier. He'd crush me like a cigarette butt under his heel. He can do anything to me.

He is silent for a while, while I try not to stare too eagerly at him for my punishment.

"So you *are* the lucky one," he says and leans forward.

I'm struck dumb. I want to hide from his gaze, penetrating and reckless as an eagle's. Eyebrows shaped like wings, so expressive in a small lift. I wish I were a painter. Or that I owned a camera. Not that I could simply photograph him. He'd ask why. "*Herr Leutnant*?"

He glances at the Messerschmitt sitting next to us like a third person. "What have you done to her?"

"I did an engine check, replaced the canopy. I . . ." I reach into my pocket and pull out the bullet I found stuck in his seat. It must have missed his shoulder by no more than a thumb's breadth when he twisted in his seat to look out for enemy planes—the shoulder that now moves in his uniform as he reaches out. I've offered the bullet without meaning to. I don't want to drop it into his hand. So he takes my wrist and I nearly jump again. But I don't let go of the bullet. He turns my palm in his to have a better look at it. "I was wondering where it went."

I can't even think. *Leutnant* Baldur Vogt is holding my hand. I'm holding something that almost killed him. Well, wounded him. Missed him, in any case. I can't free my hand to turn it and relinquish the bullet. I want to. But I don't.

He glances at me, his expression blank but somehow intent. Then his lips pull into a smile, giving me permission to breathe. I need it. "Do you want to keep it?"

My skin is hot and then cold. Why did he have to ask that? What does it mean? How to answer? My fingers are nerveless; I drop the bullet, he catches and lifts it, peers at it like a scientist would peer at a test tube. Just what is he reading in the grooves and marks on the brass surface?

I can breathe, so I breathe. "You were lucky it missed you. It was in the seat."

The *Leutnant* looks at me abruptly, drops the bullet, then catches it like somebody would catch a tossed coin. "Really? You call this lucky?"

Yes, it would have killed you. Or can you fly with a bleeding shoulder? Well enough to escape the hunters?

"I don't understand, *Herr Leutnant.*"

He scoffs. "Morbid thoughts." He glances back at the open hangar door, then stands. I don't want him to leave, even if he makes me feel like an idiot. I want to watch him smoke, I want to tell him what I did to ensure he will be as safe up there as I can make him. That I'm praying to his machine like a heathen idol to keep him alive in the clouds while I tighten every screw religiously. I can never tell him that. I don't have the words for it, either. He will think me a hero-worshipping child. If I'm lucky, he'll only laugh at me.

"Good night, *Herr Leutnant.*"

He glances at me over his shoulder. I have failed another test, but while I know what I did wrong when I failed the pilot test, I can't for the life of me understand how I failed him.

"Go to bed, Felix. I will need you fresh and awake tomorrow."

I stand to follow his order. He can't mean what he said. It's all the pilots who need me, and not just me, but the whole ground crew of six; mechanics, armourers, refuellers, two of each. With a glance, he has obliterated the others. I feel as if we are the only men alive this night, as if he is all pilots and I'm all black men. He shortens his stride, and we leave the hangar together; he's not allowing me to trail in his wake. It's almost like a conversation, walking together to the barracks. Then he separates and heads towards where the rest of his *Staffel* has to be sleeping, but stops along the way.

I pause and turn. He flicks his fingers, and I catch the bullet that comes to me in a high brass arc. His gaze is ironic, yet intent. I want to salute him, like the officer he is, although I should have done that ten minutes ago, and doing it now would be like locking the door after the burglars have walked away with the piano.

By the time I've made up my mind to pay him his due respect, he has nearly reached the barracks. I can't exactly run after him, so I tighten my fingers around the bullet. It felt like I owned it when I pulled it from his seat, like that one polished stone amidst a million on a beach that catches your attention and feels like it's meant for you alone.

He rises skyward again and again, leading one *Schwarm* of the squadron. The hour or so he spends up there on each mission, stalking, attacking, killing, protecting, draws out. He's seventy, eighty kilometres away, patrolling the skies over Berlin like an eagle protecting his nest.

Rumours of the battles travel from the control centre. When they engage the enemy, my stomach plunges and my fingers tighten around the brass cylinder in my hand. More of these are seeking their targets, and there is nothing I can do. *Leutnant* Vogt will live and die by his wits, reflexes, and cold blood alone.

Then you are the lucky one, he said.

At least his time passes in a rush, while mine . . . doesn't. An hour, sometimes more, recklessly more. Once, the squadron limped back on a breath of fumes. A few minutes longer, and they would have sailed in rather than flown. My task is to help turn the planes around as fast as possible. No time to waste as the battle goes on and command throws the fighters back into the sky in what we all know to be desperation.

This last flight is a close one. I know something is wrong from the sinking feeling in my stomach, and I know that the plane trailing smoke behind itself is Vogt's before my mind can even form the concept or make out the markings. The landing is rocky, yet the wheels hold.

The Messerschmitt swerves wildly, and we all gasp as it threatens to hurtle off the airfield and maybe topple. But it doesn't. Even with the black smoke rising from the engine, the canopy covered in oil and soot, Vogt manages to control his fate.

In my eagerness, I'm first when we rush forward to help him out of the plane. He's coughing hard when I release him from his straps, take him under his shoulders, and help to lift him out. His clear blue eyes are watery, streaming, and the acrid smoke is robbing us both of words. He's made it, and I have to let him go, care for the wounded bird, and help turn around the others.

Once this is done, I visit him in hospital. They are keeping him there just to watch him. He's inhaled smoke, but on the bed, he looks less like a patient and more like a convalescent. I'm surprised his comrades are not clamouring for his attention—or maybe they did and were shooed out. Fighter pilots are a rowdy bunch, after all. Or they can't find the time, busy as they are.

He looks up when I enter, and lowers a linen-bound green book. Herodotus's *Histories*. I remember my school days, and how I slaved over the Battle of Thermopylae. Just when I expect him to ask me why I'm there, he simply says, "Felix. Hello."

"*Herr Leutnant*," I say with all the deference he didn't get from me that first time.

He nods knowingly, then takes a postcard and marks his page with it before he closes the book. "Have a seat."

There's really only one, and I pull out the chair that occupies the space between his bed and the empty one on the other side. Sitting down, I notice him watching me. I need to speak now or I won't. And that would look strange. "It's good to see you are well." Overly familiar, but I can't hide my fear for him. He needs to know that I was worried.

Vogt nods. "The *Amis* are getting better all the time," he says, voice smoke-rough. He suppresses a cough, lines appearing around his eyes as he fights the reflex for a few moments. I reach for the pitcher they've left him and pour water into a glass and offer it. I can't help it—I'd look after the man with the same devotion I have for his plane. He takes it from my hand with a grateful nod and drinks down a deep gulp. His hair is dishevelled, blond on top, darker underneath. His expressive eyebrows curl with a frown as he concentrates on drinking.

"Are you very busy?" he asks, keeping the glass propped on his belly, supported with one hand. He's making conversation.

"A fair bit." I look down at my hands, scrubbed clean, rough from the coarse soap and working with iron, grease, and "the concentrated application of naked force," as Christensen would say. "I've been working on yours."

"How's the old lady doing?" He seems livelier now.

"She'll live," I joke, and my throat tightens when he responds with a laugh. And then a wracking cough. Damn. He lifts a hand when I lean forward, then hits his chest lightly with a curled fist, trying to dislodge the cough. "I'm sorry."

He shakes his head and rubs the water from his eyes. "Not your fault. I did down the *Ami* who did this." He leans back, deflated. Every now and then, a breath catches and threatens to turn into another cough, but it doesn't happen for a few moments. Maybe not because he's silent.

"I just meant to check in, see . . ." I shrug instead of finishing the sentence. *See how you are doing.*

He nods. "Can't wait to get back into the thick of it."

I nod too, as if I understand why. Honour, maybe. Now, so close to the end, it can't be orders. It's more than that, but I wonder what drives him skywards. The need to protect, to fight, or simply to fly? I've overheard other pilots, and while they talk about many things, they don't talk about this. Were I a pilot, what would drive me back up there?

"Where are you from?"

I blink, stutter, "Potsdam," then hurry to add, "but my parents are staying with family near Fulda." It's much safer, nestled away in the forests and with farms so close. Surely, the enemy can't bomb every single house in Germany. Surely?

"Neustadt," he says, uninvited. "I'll be going home for the weekend." I glance at his fingers, but I've never seen him wear a ring. Maybe he's not married for similar reasons as my friend Otto, the other mechanic. Who marries during war, with the rationing and shortages and most men serving in one way or another? Better to leave a grieving girl than a grieving widow.

"Just a couple of hours on the train," I offer. Fulda is a lot further, so I'm not taking time off. It feels like such a waste of time to interrupt work that seems so necessary. No wonder I almost speak more to planes than to people.

He nods. "You could come with me."

I stare at him, then shake my head. "That . . ."

"Gather strength before the end," he says, voice hushed. "The end will be bad enough."

I glance over my shoulder, worried sick that somebody heard that. Defeatism is sedition. Men get court-martialled and shot for that attitude.

His lips quirk. "You're not going to denounce me, are you?"

"No, *Herr Leutnant*." This daredevil. This maniac. "No." No. Never.

He sighs and relaxes against his pillow, as if finally convinced he is in friendly company. "You should come with me. Get away for a few days."

I'm about to protest or make excuses. I can't simply go away with him and I can't leave my post. What would people think? If I were a pilot, one of his comrades, it would be a different matter, but I'm a stranger to him, and he to me, though I can tell his style from every other pilot out there. The way he lands and takes off. I know exactly how he flies.

"I don't think they'll let me," I say, to pass on the responsibility to the Powers that Be. I want him to go—he should have time to get the smoke out of his lungs, but he can do that on his own. I'll look after the plane while he's gone.

His lips curve again in that reckless expression. *You'll see,* that smile says.

He's still coughing on the train. Unsure what we can or should say, we're both reading, he the Herodotus, I the newspapers, against my better judgment. Just a few weeks ago, we were "winning the war." Now, though, propaganda has become resigned, accusatory, as if all the losses and destruction are our fault. Even the authorities cannot uphold appearances. Reality is too stark, whispers too pervasive.

A friend of Vogt's picks us up at the train station in Neustadt. It's a small town and must have been very pretty before the war, but now it's half rubble. Burnt beams sticking out of smashed bricks like gravestones of houses. Vogt's friend tells us that city hall and the hospital are gone. More than three hundred dead. Vogt's jaw tightens, and I know what he's thinking. As much as the defenders try, they can't be everywhere, unlike the enemy. I say nothing, hoping the bombers won't reach my family hidden away in the forests. I know the place where my parents are. Ten houses, built of wood, nested against a hillside—what counts as a village in those parts. My mother's sister is married to a gamekeeper; they will even get plenty of fresh meat if my past visits are anything to go by.

When Vogt opens the door of his house—it's still standing, despite two houses hit at the start of the street—there's nothing but silence. I assumed there would be family to welcome him back, yet the place is quiet and still.

He drops in on the neighbour and returns with a basket of food covered with a red-and-white chequered kitchen towel. Day-old buns, butter wrapped in waxed paper, liver-red strawberry jam in a glass jar secured with a rubber band, a thin side of ham, some eggs with the occasional feather still clinging to them, and beer in stein bottles. I doubt whoever bought this used Vogt's ration card.

He pauses for a moment, gazes down at the towel, and we might be thinking the same—that it looks, from the corner of the eye, like blood-spattered cloth. The pattern is too regular, however, and the whole ordered madness of war is in dissolution everywhere else, so it can't live in that basket.

He makes me sit in the kitchen while he cracks eggs and cuts ham and tosses both into a heavy iron skillet. My fingers itch. I should be doing this, although the fact that I'm his guest already challenges the rank difference between us. He is not a man who sits still easily, so I watch him move, watch him suppress a cough every now and then. All the while wondering what we can talk about.

"Why did you fail the test?" he asks eventually.

It doesn't sting anymore that I did. I'm not made out of the same stuff he is. I'm content where I am and with what I'm doing. "I crashed a machine."

"Did you?" He turns around and grins. "Why?"

"I lost my nerve, was confused . . ." And crashed the training plane.

"Were you court-martialled?"

"Yes, but I was innocent. They still suggested strongly that I wasn't good enough, so I became ground crew."

"I've crashed two." He stirs the bubbling egg-and-ham mixture in the pan as white steam rises and spreads the first smell of food through the room. "Bailed once over Malta, once in Russia. Malta was a complete loss, but in Russia we salvaged the engine and the instruments. Damn sight luckier than my *Katschmarek*."

His wingman. I swallow against something in my throat and am not sure if it's fear or nervousness. "What happened?"

"He came down behind the Russian line. Took ground fire. We were battle pilots."

Engaging enemy formations low over the ground, spooking men and horses, and throwing bombs from a low altitude. I look at him, try to read his features, but his eyes are unfocused, staring into a distance the dark kitchen doesn't yield.

"We were circling and watched the Russians get to him. They beat him to death with the butts of their rifles where he stood, hands raised."

"What did you do?"

"Machine-gunned the lot," he says and shakes his head. "We'd heard that the war in the east was different. No gentleman's agreement, no honour, all rules of war thrown into the fire."

"I'm sorry to hear."

He smiles. "I'd rather fight the *Amis* or Tommies. Haven't seen any of them beat a prisoner to death. Maybe it's only a matter of time now." He turns back and serves the eggs and ham onto two plates, then puts one in front of me. "But Berlin is far in the east."

I take the plate and pull it closer. Thinking of Russian tanks in Berlin makes me feel ill. Somehow, my mind was always too exhausted to think that far until now. We all know defeat is coming, or maybe a truce just in time to save us all, though the Führer will never yield. Nobody can imagine him petitioning for peace. Short of all the angels of the Lord descending from heaven to fight on our side, there's just no other way this war can go.

My mind usually freezes before I reach that point in my thoughts. I keep busy just to not think about it. I can fix an engine, reload and fuel a plane—I can't fix this war. I'm not sure I'd want to. Maybe the Nazis aren't that wrong in leading us all to Ragnarök. Maybe they are right, and living as slaves is a fate worse than death. Maybe Germany *did* squander her chance at greatness. Maybe something will happen that stops the end from coming just in time.

I tuck in, my body too used to eating when it can and sleeping when it can to allow such thoughts to ruin a good meal. Vogt pulls a bun apart and watches me with interest.

"Why am I here?" I ask as I scrape the last few morsels together, then wipe them up with a piece of bread.

"You said your family is too far away to visit on leave."

"Like yours?"

He shakes his head. "We don't speak."

"Why?"

"My father lost his business because I wasn't there to take over." He collects the plates, clearly restless to be doing things.

At the rate at which he's been flying, I doubt he's found any rest recently. From briefing to mission to debriefing and yet another briefing and mission until weather and light and naked exhaustion put a stop to the relentless rhythm . . . No wonder he can't sit still. They haven't let him for a while, and even with the smoke still burning his lungs, I can see that he thinks he should be doing something. Maybe it was a bad idea to come here at all. His *Staffel* is going to miss him, and definitely *Hauptmann* Wischinsky, the captain of the squadron.

Maybe that's what he thinks, that he should be out there, leading his men and supporting his captain in one of those many attacks. He's emanating restlessness, uneasiness, and I hate to think I'm the one thing holding him back from where he'd rather be. We're both at loose ends without the machine that connects us, however furtively.

"What's on your mind?"

I inhale deeply. "Just wondering why I'm here."

"I wanted to thank you."

And for that, you've dragged me away from the airfield? I smile, but don't really look at him. "Least I can do if I can't fly."

"You still pulled me out."

He's right, so I shrug. I don't want to admit to the childish fancies I have about him. For me, he can walk on water, dance in the clouds. I know he can't, really, but what he can and can't do pales into nothing when I look at him. Something pulls me towards him, irrespective of the impossibility of it all. I hope that he doesn't notice just as much as I hope that he's pulled, too. What am I compared to a wingman he protects and who protects him, who knows what it is like to soar? Compared to comrades who stood by him in Russia? I merely maintain engines, change oil, and help with the other tasks, dirty, exhausting, and not glorious at all.

"I'm glad I did."

"So am I." Vogt looks solemn.

This house is too big for us—it seems to loom in the darkness, filled with furniture that has lived in strangers' memories. This isn't home, and I'm dreading closing my eyes here. I want to go home, or at least to a place where I'm among my own kind. Wherever that is.

We settle somewhat uneasily in the living room. Vogt cleans a layer of dust from the piano in the corner, but doesn't touch the keys. Unplayed sound is like unspoken words. He turns back to me just as I'm about to make my excuses and ask to be shown to my room.

"I did notice your face under the oil."

I can't suppress the urge to rub at my cheek with one—clean—hand. He makes me feel like an ash-covered Cinderella. I watch him, wondering where this will lead. I stifle a yawn, and whatever he was about to say next, he smiles instead and leads me to my room.

I set my bag down, and I expect him to say goodnight. "You know, a friend of mine told me a story about the black men in his wing." He pauses, but I don't offer anything. Who knows what pilots say about us amongst themselves?

"One commander was concerned that the black men looked untidy when Wolfram von Richthofen came in for an inspection. *Baron* von Richthofen. So he has the pilots stand at attention, and the ground crew assemble behind a shed, hoping he won't see them. But von Richthofen does, of course, and asks who do those men belong to. So the commander has to admit they belong to his wing, and von Richthofen tells the ground crew to come forward and take their rightful place. The Baron didn't think for a moment that they looked out of place next to all the crisp and clean pilots."

Told by one of ours, this story would have gone differently. I get what he's saying—that we belong to the wing, just as essential to it as the iron and steel without which a pilot is merely a soldier staring longingly into heaven. I *knew* that. That he has to tell the story at all leaves a strange taste in my mouth.

He means well. He's being generous. In some odd way, he means to tell me we're comrades, even maybe, possibly, equals. That he feels like he has to say it betrays that we're not, to his mind.

"Goodnight, Felix," he says when I don't really respond. I don't think he expected much more from me. So why do I feel like I should have said something when I close the door?

The bed is cold despite the heavy feather-stuffed duvet. It takes a long time before the mattress gives up the clammy chill that I imagine settled in here while the house was deserted. How long has Vogt been flying—half noble protector, half avenging angel—and not come home? Pilots are hell-raisers off duty, spending their pay without thoughts of tomorrow. Lately, the thought of tomorrow is like the thought of a hundred years into the future. Who can imagine that Germany will still exist?

I've been too harsh on him. He dragged me out here for company because, for whatever reason, his comrades in his squadron wouldn't do. He needed a stranger, somebody on the periphery of the flying circus. Maybe he'd felt comfortable, sharing that cigarette.

I did notice your face under the oil.

I touch my fingertips to my cheek, trace the skin there, touch the corner of my mouth. Maybe I resent him because he is what I failed to become. I'm the eagle who died in his egg while my brother grew up strong and proud.

You're the lucky one.

Now I can't sleep, although the mattress is finally warm. I push my legs out from under the covers and get dressed again, shivering in the night chill crawling into the house. I leave the guest room and walk downstairs. There's soft golden light under the door to the living room, and I push it open without knocking.

He's sitting at the piano, a snifter of cognac standing naked on the highly polished wood. He's bowed deep over the keys, fingers silently tapping them, not pressing hard enough to make any sound. A silent music only he can hear, and whatever he's hearing, it's slow and deliberate and terribly melancholic. And, the strangest thing is, I can almost hear it too.

The sudden realisation chokes off my next breath. I must have made a sound, because he straightens and turns around, a thin strand of his straight hair falling onto his forehead with a rakish air. His expression is contemplative, but not, I notice, surprised. I want to move away, back into his blind spot. I want to tell him what I feel when I see him take to the skies, and what I felt when he trailed the dark smoke behind him. How I'd hoped he wouldn't have to bail to avoid being burned alive, because at that altitude, his parachute wouldn't have opened in time. And I simply wouldn't have been able to see him die on that airfield.

"I don't know why I care so much, but I do," I finally admit.

His fingers touch the keys, gently, as if he were getting to know the piano. "I can see that in your face." He bends his neck. "You watch me."

You must be watching me too if you can tell that. "Like right now, you mean?" I'm forgetting my place. We are not exactly friends or familiar in any other way. But I care. We could know each other, if any man can ever know a hero.

His lips twitch, then he suppresses another cough and spreads his fingers out on the keys, depressing them a little, still making no sound. With his manic energy, I'd expect Beethoven from him, though right now he looks like someone contemplating Chopin.

"So, you couldn't sleep?" he asks. "Cognac?"

"Yes. Yes, please."

He straightens up and walks to the cabinet, then pours me the same drink he's having and brings it back to me. I take the glass from his hand and sip. The alcohol is as strong as it is mellow—this is expensive stuff, something for celebrations rather than quaffing in a *Kneipe*. He smiles at me. He's taller than I am from this close.

"Unfamiliar sounds?" he asks.

"No sounds at all. I'm not used to the quiet."

He nods. "Always takes me a few days."

I'm so thrilled to have found more common ground than the steel and oil and danger that I almost forget about the alcohol. I'm a fool, a hero-worshipping fool. My more critical facilities know that Vogt isn't a saviour; he's one of many, like any soldier ready to die for the Fatherland. And yet, I've chosen him to be special for me.

But why? It's not simply his looks. He caught my eye first when he was standing with his squadron-mates on the airfield. There was Wolff, his *Katschmarek,* a friendly, broad-faced boy from Hamburg with black hair; and Simon, who sounds Southern, agitated, loud, and gifted with infectious humour. There's Wischinsky, East Prussian, of course, high cheekbones, pale face with wide blue eyes, aloof, wide-framed, tossing out verbal barbs and ending conversations as easily as Simon starts them.

And then Vogt, standing just a step apart from the others. It felt like it was an effort for him to really be part of their group. That is how I sometimes feel. Like him, I belong by virtue of my training and my duty; I'm one of the black men, part of an always-frantic brotherhood. Yet just like him, there's one thing I cannot bridge, cannot overcome.

He comes closer, leaning in or inching closer, I can't tell. I'm wholly taken by his eyes and the faint outline of a vein on the left side of his brow. I blink and answer his gaze, which is intent and focused, as if he's searching the sky for a deadly foe. Or a target. It's really both, and between us now, too.

Oddly, I expect him to kiss me. My heart somersaults and then plummets, but it never crashes; that pressure like nausea remains unbroken, until I'm nearly ready to beg him to do something. He lifts a hand and slides his fingers along my temple, as if he were pushing back a strand of hair. But my hair isn't long enough for that. I stare at him, swallow, then his fingers trail down my temple, that soft, soft skin between cheek and ear, and then track my jawline. At my chin, his fingers change direction and trace the other side of my face. I 'm hypnotised. Entranced.

"Are you guessing it by now?" he asks, his voice so low, as if there were other people in the room who must never know.

Swallowing is painful now. I'm busy enough just with breathing. I feel astutely that this is the only opportunity I'll ever have to risk everything, neck and life and sanity.

If the world ends tomorrow, how will I go? Without ever having risked anything, or having done the one thing I can't stop thinking about? His eyes are mild, generous. Is that trust? I take his hand, notice his skin isn't entirely dry, and neither is mine. I straighten somewhat, then stare at his lips.

And that's when I kiss him.

My heart is still plunging, but the other sensations are strong enough to make me forget about the nausea. His lips are softer than I imagined them. He's not wrestling for control. Neither is he demanding anything. The kiss is sweet, gentle, out of place. He lifts his eyebrows and puts a hand against my neck; the other hand squeezes mine, and I squeeze back. I'm no longer falling—I'm soaring now, breathless and miraculous, weightless. As if a wide blue sky has opened for me, like in the best moments of my glider training. I can't believe we're doing this. He's holding my hand, touching my neck. Seems reluctant to release me.

I pull away, clear my throat. I can't believe I kissed him.

He smiles and lets my neck go, but keeps my hand in his. "Not something that's suitable for the airfield."

The thought is outrageous, scandalous, and I can't suppress an amused snort. "I didn't think . . ." So many things I don't want to say. It would all sound weird and as if I were making assumptions, when I'm just speechless and overwhelmed.

"That I'd seen you?"

"That, and . . ." I want to kick myself for being so tongue-tied. I soldier on, pride be damned. "That you would kiss . . . a man."

He laughs, and I decide then and there that I love how he laughs, a short burst of mirth that would look forced or staged on anybody else.

"My dear Felix, situation allowing, I even find my special friends a decent meal and gifts."

Special friends. Is that what he calls such arrangements between men? I'm clueless. It's not exactly the blood brotherhood of my adventure stories, where men die for each other without ever kissing. "Where did you do that?"

"There was a boy in Paris. French. He seemed rather experienced in some ways." Vogt winks at me. "Don't look at me like that. It's been five years."

I shake my head, put my glass down. "No, I . . . I've never had a friend like that."

"Never?"

"I kissed a friend when I was very young, but we grew out of it."

Vogt touches my face again. "But you didn't."

"No. I missed him, but I understood that it's dangerous." But then, the world may end tomorrow.

He nods and kisses me again. It's a heartfelt yet tender kiss that makes my pulse race. I reach to grab his shoulder, still reluctant to let his hand go, and he doesn't free himself. We stand there and just kiss, and with every touch, we seem to explain and apologise, and bridge that gap that yawned between us. After a while, I feel like I know him, and my heart turns to liquid at the thought that this courageous warrior has called me his friend. Who am I to be worthy of him?

He guides me to the couch, where we sit close together. He pulls my head closer still, and kisses my ear.

"Go on. You're safe and sound here with me," he whispers.

I calm down. Before long, I'm half asleep against his shoulder. He finds a woollen blanket and we rest together, wrapped up against the cool night.

I've never felt so at peace with anybody, and while I'm bone-weary, I'm alive with him here, our bodies touching with so much ease, so much trust and familiarity. We don't know each other, but I know we're not judging one another, not making any demands, just enjoying the moment. I'm dimly aware that he stretches out and takes his shoes off, and soon I'm resting halfway on his chest, feeling him breathe, one arm slung around me. The exhaustion has caught up with me, yet I relish these minutes that turn into hours. I sleep, maybe two or three hours before a touch against my hair wakes me.

I jerk away with a start, but Vogt tightens his grip against my shoulder and keeps me there. "Easy."

I nod and push away with more care, then rub at my eyes. "I slept."

"Seemed you needed it, too," he says. "Let's move to the bedroom." We sit up, and I gather the woollen blanket and fold it before I follow him upstairs. Without so much as a glance, he gestures for me to follow him to his room.

It's dark apart from some moonlight seeping through the shutters, and I don't want to switch on the light. I undress, too apprehensive to walk away and dress in my pyjamas and come back.

We slip into his bed like a married couple. I know he is naked, and the night chill makes me shiver. The bed will get warm soon, though now it feels quite cold against naked skin. He pushes himself up on an elbow and kisses my lips again. Oh. I can't resist and run my hand down his chest, feel the muscles shift under his skin. I take the sound he makes as encouragement.

He brushes my leg, and then I can't hold back anymore and run my fingers through the wiry hair of his groin, where I encounter his prick. Vogt moans against my lips as I touch him carefully, then playfully, and then with more courage. I want to learn his body, find every pleasure it's hiding. All this reverence and simple awe I feel when I touch him, feel his breath brush my skin. Whatever he calls this, it feels so very precious to me.

"Felix," he whispers. "Can I do something?"

"Anything."

I see the outline of his smile in the near dark, and then he touches me, fingers sure on my flesh. I lose myself in the moment, in his touch, push into his hand and kiss him hungrily when he turns my head towards him again. This feels like a gift I barely deserve. Or maybe I do, even though I don't know what for. I haven't done anything.

He rolls on top of me, kisses me again, then manoeuvres himself into position alongside me. His strong hand holds us together, and he moves to pleasure us both. I can't do much more than thrust against him and cling to his shoulders. I want to feel all of this, to be swept up in the moment, and he lets me. There's nothing I'm supposed to be doing, merely kissing him and moving with him, feeling all the strength in his body and the heat and desire I sense through every jerky movement and every breathless kiss.

We race towards something so amazing and precious it strikes me dumb with its immenseness. I lose every sense of myself, every thought; there's just emotion and utter fulfilment.

We breathe heavily against each other for a long time after, until he touches my face again and gives me another kiss. Then he lies down beside me, offering me his shoulder. I turn and nestle up against him. The bed is much warmer now, although wetness runs off my belly. I'm tired, at peace, and I can't leave the place on his shoulder, not after I've found it.

"Sleep well," he murmurs into my ear.

I just hope he'll be there when I wake up.

I've never woken to another's body in the same bed, not since I was a child. There is something about it that makes waking up alone seem unnatural. Man is not meant to be alone, yet men like us (or maybe men like me) appear to be lonelier than others. I watch his face in the morning light, and notice an occasional furrowing of his brow, as if he is focusing on something out there in his dreamscape. Maybe he's flying even in his dreams, searching the skies for signs of an ambush.

I contemplate the prospect of breakfast. I'm ravenous, but this is a strange place and I'm not sure where the shops are, or his ration card. Snooping around the house does not seem as enticing as watching him. Eventually, I lean in and kiss him on the lips, just to confirm I still have the nerve for it.

He smiles and wakes with a stretch, then opens his eyes. "Have you been awake long?"

"No, just a little while." I don't know, don't particularly care about timekeeping outside the rhythm of work on the airfield.

He runs the backs of his fingers down the side of my face. The touch is sleep-warm, a little clumsy, as he drags himself awake.

"Look at that, it was no dream."

For that, I kiss him again, and he pulls me closer. I look down at him, thrilled that we are both naked.

"I promised my aunt I'd visit her when I'm home," he says, interrupting all considerations of what to do with the morning that doesn't involve getting up. "She'll feed us, too."

"Does she know you're bringing a friend?"

"By now, people know. It's a small town." He gets up and gathers his clothes, taking them to the bathroom as he leaves. "You'll have to call me by my first name, or she'll ask questions," he says over his shoulder.

His name puts me in mind of Ragnarök, the end of the world, again—Baldur, the god whose death sets the spiral of destruction in motion that none of the other gods can stop. Baldur the bright, Baldur the brave. It feels like a bad omen.

When he's done in the bathroom, I go in to get washed and dressed and shaved, taking my time, unlike in the mad rush of duty. I remember all too well cutting myself badly one morning when I was too bleary-eyed to do a good job of it. Christensen laughed at me, but still sent me to get patched up so I wouldn't bleed on the engines. The scar is noticeable enough to remind me not to be hasty around blades.

Baldur is wearing his dress uniform when we go down the street and turn left, left again, straight on, to his aunt's house.

It's a large, handsome farmhouse with a well-tended garden in the front. His aunt is much older than I expect; his uncle is gruff and lost a leg in the previous war against the French. I understand he is Baldur's blood relation—his aunt has married into the family.

Baldur speaks of the airfield, but not candidly. If I believed his words and didn't know better, I'd be left with an idea of adventure rather than war, or challenge rather than danger. She looks at him with a haunted expression, and his uncle, a retired officer, calls the Führer a "criminally insane lowlife upstart," once, under his breath, yet nothing comes of it. There isn't even real ire in those words; it is an argument that has long since been won, and Baldur's uncle states it merely as a matter of course.

There is much admiration, however, for Baldur's decorations (I still struggle to call him that, after months of "*Leutnant* Vogt"), and I feel oddly proud although I haven't won a thing and never even helped him win them.

Nobody speaks of the end. I assume they are heartily sick of the subject, or push those thoughts far away. Baldur's aunt once wipes her hands on her apron and mutters, "Well, well, nobody could have foreseen it would come to this," with a tone halfway between indignation and apology. I keep mostly silent unless Baldur requires a nod or a confirmation for his own short anecdotes—nothing too grisly or honest, just the silly little things that seem to happen on an airfield regardless of how the war is going.

I feel like a sad clown when we finally take our leave, having barely fended off an attempt to foist more food on us. We will be leaving tomorrow; Baldur is fine, and neither of us has any excuse to not be at his post.

We do attack the cognac when we get home. Baldur takes off his gloves and sits down at the piano. After not having been played in a while, some notes might very well be off, but I'm more entranced by the man in the uniform who begins fluidly, then falters, trying to remember a passage. He takes off his hat and places it on the piano to try again, from the start, with gusto.

I pour more cognac for both of us and stand near the piano with my glass and the bottle, watching his face as he struggles through playing a classical piece. His half-closed eyes and bared teeth make him look fierce and absorbed in the task, and I imagine that is what he looks like during a complicated manoeuvre.

He breaks off and slaps the keys. "Damn it. I can't remember!" He blows out a breath and looks at me. "I haven't played in six years."

"After six years, I'd barely remember which part of the piano to sit down at," I joke and offer him the glass.

He takes my wrist instead and pulls me down on the seat before the piano. "Have you ever played?"

Upon my admission that, no, I haven't, he puts me through an improvised lesson that is as excruciating as it is funny. The piano doesn't sound like it approves of my attempts, and by the time we're through the bottle, we're reduced to helpless laughter. I don't even care that we're laughing at my lack of nimbleness or talent. Just the laughter means elation, a lessening of the pressure mounting on us, a pressure that will have us back tomorrow and the day after and for however long it'll take. With the things Baldur is facing once he returns, I don't mind him laughing at me.

He turns serious and kisses me again, his taste of cognac mixing with my taste of the same cognac, and within moments we're both stretched out on the Persian carpet, the piano's leg close to our faces.

"This would mean some work before we can play together," he says, grinning.

Can, not *could*, I hear, and understand. I rub my eyes. "Since we can't fly together." I'm making light of what he said, but I guess I can have my revenge this way.

"I wouldn't want you up there." He looks into my eyes intently. "It's bad enough that my friends are up there."

He doesn't understand what I feel when I see him take off, then. "Tell me about your Frenchman."

"Jacques?" He rolls over onto his back and pulls me to his shoulder. "He wasn't mine or anybody's. We met a few times for a while, but he was a hard-working lad from Ménilmontant, one of the poorer parts of Paris. We met on the street one day; he smiled at me, I smiled back, and suddenly he took my arm and we walked for a while. I assumed he was a rentboy, but he wasn't." Baldur shrugs. "He was looking for diversion; I was looking for company, though I didn't expect to find any, certainly not with an enemy. But he was too young to have fought against us and didn't seem to bear anybody ill will. Then my squadron was moved to the Eastern front, and we lost contact. It was tenuous anyway. Just shared meals and companionship, and little gifts that wouldn't have bought the attentions of anyone who was looking to receive gifts for favours."

It is the most I've ever heard him speak. I try to imagine him in his uniform with his medals and finery—like he is now—trading kisses with a worker lad. "What did you do with him?"

"I took him cycling outside the city. Or we'd walk in the park. Some evenings, we'd go to a music hall for a drink and to listen to the singers. There was one entertainer—they called him the Nightingale of Paris—who had the most amazing voice. I think Jacques was very fond of him." Baldur chuckles. "He was very pretty too, but I think one of the high-ranking *Wehrmacht* officers had already staked his claim. That's Paris for you—so decadent she even conquers the conquerors with her wiles." He rolls his eyes as he quotes the official propaganda. "I'd like to go back, though. Nobody cares there what you're doing, and we could do things much more openly. I've heard of many such arrangements."

"You mean, after the war?"

He looks at me, suddenly much more serious. "Maybe in another life."

The sense of foreboding presses the air from my lungs. I'm falling again, but it's not my place to add to his burden with my fear. I grab him and press his face against my chest, and his hands squeeze under my shoulders and hold me close. I don't know what to do with myself, but at least I don't cry. Not while he's still alive.

Getting home—I mean, to the airfield—takes longer than usual. The Allied bombers have wreaked havoc on a train depot.

Our train is rerouted, and we pass through a town—I know not which one—that is still burning. Thick smoke rises and lingers like fog. Baldur coughs into a handkerchief as he peers outside, searching the skies above us for attackers. It is harder and harder to ignore the destruction all around us. Especially for Baldur, who's been tasked to stop the perpetrators before they reach their targets. We both know the *Luftwaffe* is outgunned. I glance at the book on his lap. Still Herodotus.

Nervous tension fills me, so I close my eyes and remember how we were together last night. The kisses, the tenderness, the relief, all suspended in time. If only I could fight by his side, I wouldn't feel as helpless as I do now.

When we arrive at the airfield, he is greeted by his *Staffelkameraden*, and I join the ranks of the other mechanics. They say "welcome back," and I am on the next shift right away because I don't know what else to do with myself while he's gone.

The next morning, I see the pilots stride across the airfield to their machines. They are ready to go yet again, and I climb onto Baldur's machine when he slides into the cockpit. I strap him in quickly, and smile briefly at him. It's not out of the ordinary at all. I don't look at him, just at the straps I buckle, and then I close the canopy for him. While he does a radio check, I start his engine. The others pull the chocks from the wheels, and the squadron rolls down the airfield, moving in perfect unison, the drone of the engines sounding back to us before each *Rotte* pair rises and lifts up into the sky.

That day, his squadron flies four more sorties, and the rush and pressure of activity on the airfield is the only distraction I get. Every time he lands, I'm the first at his machine, but the others follow closely after, so there's no opportunity even for a word. I may get a reputation as some kind of faithful hound to him, but he smiles at me when he climbs out, pats my shoulder before he joins his squadron mates to be debriefed.

One evening, as I'm working by myself on a Stuka dive bomber engine in the back of the hangar, he comes closer. I recognise his shape from the corner of my eye, but I can't stop my work with both arms up to the elbows in steel and iron and grease. I've made good progress on this during my free time, tinkering away to revive the plane, even if it might end up being used for spare parts.

He pauses a few steps away, and I grimace and then grin at him. "Just a moment." I finish oiling the engine and pull my arms, covered in soot and grease, free. I wipe at my fingers with a rag, even knowing that cleaning them is futile without a generous quantity of soap.

Baldur offers me a cigarette and lights it when I nod. He slips it between my lips so I don't have to touch it. I inhale deeply and push the cigarette into one corner of my mouth.

"Why are you still working?" he asks softly.

"Trying to get this bird back into the air as soon as possible." I shrug over at the Stuka whose heart I'm operating on right now.

He places a hand on my shoulder and squeezes. I want to lean into him, hug him close, but I'm too concerned about blackening him all up. That would be difficult to explain.

"I didn't want to do that to you, Felix."

I toss the oily rag on the ground. "What?"

"I don't want you to fear for me. I shouldn't have revealed myself to you."

And carry the burden alone? Oh, this is precious. "It didn't make any difference," I hiss, and he's clearly taken aback. "All you did was show me that my stupid longing had hope of fulfilment." I'm angry and I don't even know why. He looks stricken, so I take a step closer. "And I still do. You've returned so far, and if it has anything to do with me, you will *keep* coming back."

His gaze flickers to the engine. "Nothing short of witchcraft," he mutters.

I spit out the cigarette and grab him by the collar, his Knight's Cross digging into my raw knuckles as I do. I want to rail at him, but somehow, we end up kissing. The despair tastes like machine oil, thick and heavy, something nobody can swallow. It's madness, and worse madness that neither of us fights the other off. He should push me away, and I shouldn't have kissed him in the first place.

I catch a movement from the corner of my eye, and I see another pilot staring at us. It's the tall pale Prussian, Wischinsky, Baldur's squadron leader. I jerk away as if from an engine still hot from battle, wishing the ground would swallow me up. Baldur straightens and wipes his mouth, peers at his hand, no doubt to check if my dirt and oil have transferred to him. I'm mortified, speechless with the possible consequences. The last thing I wanted to do was dishonour him.

Baldur inhales deeply, expands his chest, and faces his superior officer. I just shrink away and peer at the man whose pale face betrays nothing in the shadow cast by his cap.

"*Leutnant* Vogt," he snaps, eventually.

Baldur straightens up further, if that were even possible.

"You were missed," he says, and his words might be friendly and refer to the squadron doing something together while Baldur had stolen away to see me. My heart had surely stopped and now races to make up for lost beats.

Baldur casts me a warning glance and follows his superior officer out of the hangar. I sit down, weak with relief and dread. I can't even say which one is stronger. Everything depends now on what Baldur can explain. Maybe Wischinsky didn't actually see us. The pause before he addressed Baldur was too meaningful for me to hope that is true. Maybe Baldur can talk him out of whatever disciplinary action he is contemplating. They are both heroes, after all, *Experten*, veterans of many years.

I spend minutes just calming my shaking fingers and smoking in silence, but it does nothing to settle my nerves.

I watch Wischinsky closely. When he walks to and from his plane, he's every centimetre the decorated flying ace. Baldur once complained that Wischinsky enjoys the duel more than accomplishing an objective. He also never warns his squadron before he takes an action, often breaks out of formation to chase a British or American pilot when the opportunity arises.

"He acts like we're still on the offensive. The godforsaken fool will get us all killed," Baldur snarled once when he dropped from the cockpit.

To Baldur's one hundred and forty kills, Wischinsky adds another sixty-four—both are legends in their own right. Yet Wischinsky is a *Condor Legion* veteran, and a test pilot for prototypes that never made it into production. He's considered the wing's best acrobat in the sky, and he invented manoeuvres before he asked to be sent back to the front, whereas Baldur has only ever been a fighter pilot, if a very good one.

I know it's a competition between them, a friendly rivalry, with Baldur challenging his superior and attempting to live up to the more experienced warrior who continues to put him in his place with displays of skill alone. Though Wischinsky bears the Knight's Cross of the Iron Cross with Oak Leaves and Swords, one of the highest possible decorations, I've never seen him pull rank on anybody. Maybe he really just loves flying, the chase and the kill—maybe he is a reluctant leader of men, elevated for his skills and ability far beyond his comfort. Of course, now he is also a very real danger for us, though I struggle to think of how he can punish us. We can't be sent to the Eastern Front, for example. The Eastern Front is now just outside Berlin. At night, I can hear artillery boom and thunder, and it's not ours.

The fighting gets more desperate, too. Fewer machines return, and I've used up almost all my spare engine parts. We're running low on everything—parts, but most of all fuel. We're all working to exhaustion, and I almost dare hope that Wischinsky's forgotten the disciplinary matter. What evil have we done? Nothing. We've barely exchanged glances ever since, Baldur too busy fighting, and the only thing that keeps me from being driven out of my mind is more work, harder work, and tinkering on the Stuka when my usual work is done, restoring the useless plane because only utter exhaustion gets me to sleep.

One day, the squadron returns without Simon. They saw him explode in mid-air, high up, and none of them spotted the white plume of his parachute. It does not mean he's dead, says Wolff, but they are all sombre, as if at a funeral. The absence of Simon's riotous laughter weighs twice as heavy, and in our hearts we all know he's dead.

And to make matters worse, Wischinsky receives bad news just a few hours later, as he steps from his plane. He's called to the side, where an aide hands him a letter. He opens it then and there, impatient, reads it quickly. It can only be a few lines of text.

Then I see something I never expected to see. The tall man staggers as if struck by lightning, and covers his face. For several moments he stands there, all alone, then he lifts his hands away and folds the letter, pushes it into his uniform and leaves for the barracks.

Several hours later, the news has made the rounds. Wischinsky's wife and two small children were killed during an air raid on Berlin. I feel terrible for having been afraid of him and what he might do to us.

If anything, people work harder and more diligently around Wischinsky now, a silent, barely visible way to express our support and condolences.

The alarms sound again, warning us of inbound enemy aircraft. Wischinsky runs towards his plane, where we are all ready to help him get off the ground as fast as humanly possible. He doesn't look at any of us, merely climbs into his cockpit, steers out to the airfield, and takes off to lead his squadron into battle. Simon is replaced by the sole survivor of another squadron.

Baldur flies with them, and this time, when I strap him in, he does something he's never done before. He presses a letter into my hand, which is wrapped around something hard and angular. I recognise it by touch the moment I see he's missing his Knight's Cross, and I want to rail at him, but there's no time, and it's not the place. Short of giving everything away, the whole messy pain of this, and baring it to the world that is now in its death throes, I can't do a thing but my duty.

Like Icarus, he rises to the sky. I'm about to shed the tears that Wischinsky did not cry in public. I want to rage against fate, against the orders to keep fighting to the last man, against the madness that has darkened every mind. They say the top brass is considering suicide missions to destroy bridges and slow the Soviet advance. Maybe they already are flying such missions. What little information there is might be outdated or twisted so as not to demoralise us. Some of us run; mostly it's the civilian staff who creep away in the dead of the night to, I guess, await the end huddled with their families. The fighter pilots rise again to fight, and will fight until destroyed, I have no doubt.

When planes appear in the blue spring sky, I don't have time to breathe a sigh of relief. These aren't ours. All our pilots are gone, yet I see men scramble to the anti-aircraft guns that are now our only defence. I'm out on the airfield between the machines under maintenance, too far away from any cover. Around me, people scream and begin to run.

The Mustangs come in low, swooping like hawks to evade the flak. I see their colours, their markings. This is the closest I've ever come to the enemy.

Suddenly, there comes the throatier roar of our Messerschmitts. Did they turn around and change objectives from protecting Berlin to protecting the airfield? I don't know, but those engines are the most beautiful thing I've ever heard. Still, they are too far away.

I can't outrun a fighter plane. When an enemy pilot drops bombs on the spare Messerschmitts, all I feel is indignation. The bastard doesn't know how much work he's destroying. Then the paralysis bleeds away and I turn and run towards the barracks, though they won't withstand the attack.

Another Mustang swoops down, driving the fleeing personnel towards the machine gun of his squad mate. I freeze in terror, unwilling to run in either direction, while around me the Messerschmitts are burning.

Then one plane falls out of the sky, just simply drops. I half expect to hear the terrifying siren howl of a Stuka dive bomber, yet the plane's shape is all wrong, and I've never heard of a Stuka successfully attacking an airborne plane in a dive. It doesn't matter. The enemy doesn't see the plane coming and continues on his path.

It's happening so fast I barely comprehend what I see. The diving Messerschmitt lazily adjusts its course, and just as I believe he isn't going to do it, it crashes nose-first into the rump of the attacker. The frames distort into something beyond recognition, then in two distinct explosions both become a single fireball.

I'm knocked back as the hellish heat washes over me, ears ringing as debris rains down all around, shocked that I should escape death at such a cost.

With an angry roar, another Messerschmitt falls like an eagle on the other Mustang. Thus engaged, the enemy pilot breaks off the attack on the airfield and gains altitude before he wheels to engage the Messerschmitt in a dogfight, the higher buzz from his engine no less angry than the darker rumble of the Messerschmitt's. Even I can see that the enemy fighter is more manoeuvrable, and its pilot skilled and courageous, or he'd have long since turned tail and run from the vicious attack.

I hear the Messerschmitt's machine guns, see the enemy pilot turn to absorb the punishment, and it rather looks like two large birds of prey hissing at each other while fighting to the death. I get to my feet, feel wetness on my coveralls, and try to run while the Messerschmitt pilot fights for his life not that much higher up. I pray to every piece of the machine I've oiled and cleaned and refuelled and reloaded that we'll gain one more victory—

My knees give out. Around me is nothing but chaos and panic and smoke and fire as my vision blackens.

Pain brings the world back into focus. Somebody gathers me up like a fallen child. I feel something sticking out of my side, which hurts worse when it's jostled. A distorted piece of plane, not even that big. Part of a canopy frame?

The man carrying me is Baldur. I cry out when he hurts me. I didn't expect to see him again, but now I know that the other pilot was Wischinsky. He's flown every plane, including some that never made it into mass production, but before he became the leader of this fighter squadron, he flew Stukas.

"What . . ."

"Don't speak." Baldur runs with me across the airfield. I only see smoke and destruction, and am not altogether sure why he's carrying me to the end of the airfield. There's a plane—it's a Stuka, my Stuka, the one I've been working on for weeks. "Is it ready to fly? Fuelled up?"

I nod, weakly, half indignant that he'd even ask.

He manoeuvres me into the gunner seat, and I think I must have screamed. I feel blood run down inside my coveralls, but he helps me get my legs into the cockpit regardless of my protests. I'm hurt, and he wants to fly? It's not something I can understand. He straps me in, takes my hands, and presses them against the wound.

"Hold this. Don't you dare bleed out on me."

I want to tell him that it doesn't hurt that much. And that I'm not afraid. I've only ever really been afraid of the fear, but right now, I fear nothing. I wish the pain would stop, but that's it. After the raid I'm not the sanest I've been. I don't think he'll hold it against me.

I feel the engine start, and then we're rolling, speeding up, while smoke billows all around us. Baldur is starting blind, rolling over debris—maybe bodies, from the feel of it—but still, the dive bomber hurtles down the airfield. With a little jerk, we are skybound. I see the base rush past and become small, then we climb.

I clutch the piece of metal in my side and push as far as I can away from the cockpit wall, but every jostle, every turn hurts, and I'm not sure I can control the bleeding. There's really nothing I can use to staunch it.

I drift in and out of what passes for consciousness. In those minutes or hours, I don't care if I'm dying. I merely endure the discomfort and watch the landscape below us rush past. Judging by the shadows and the golden afternoon light, we're flying west. I turn my eyes towards the sky and feel a placid joy. I'm flying towards the sun, carried by an eagle's wings.

I hear Baldur speak, but it's all muffled. He slows, waggles his wings. He's surrendering. Then two large shadows circle us. They look like enemies—plump, cigar-shaped Thunderbolts, the most graceless fighter planes in existence—yet nobody is shooting or doing any kind of acrobatics. We're being escorted.

I wake next when the plane sets down on another airfield. It's evening now, the light is all red, the shadows long. I glance outside and see Baldur standing on a different airfield, hands raised over his head. I remember his story about his *Katschmarek* who came down behind enemy lines and was beaten to death by the *Iwans*. These soldiers don't look like Slavs. One of them is black. I've never seen a black-skinned man this close. He looks nothing like those in the caricatures or the captured French African troops they paraded around in the newsreels. They must be Americans.

After a soldier has taken Baldur's pistol and dagger away, a different soldier gestures towards me. Baldur turns and looks at me, and I nod. I see him smile, harried and exhausted, and then they lead him away.

I don't know who our captors think I am, but only one of them keeps an eye on Baldur when he comes to visit me. The guard seems to be a friendly fellow and smiles at me when I turn my head towards him.

Baldur sits at my bedside, holds my hand, and even smiles. To our captors, I'm the man he's taken to safety behind enemy lines. Maybe they think we're just comrades. They can't think we're brothers; they've seen my *Soldbuch*, which lists my name and rank and unit and pay. No doubt they've processed Baldur as a prisoner of war, too.

"How are you feeling?" he asks eventually.

I nod and squeeze his hand lightly. So many things I want to say, how the luxury of lying flat on my back is spoiled by the odd urge that I should be working. Or that I can see that his eyes are haunted, and I wonder whether he is thinking of Wischinsky or Simon, or even his friend who died in Russia. Most of all, though, I'm grateful that he's returned, unlike the others.

"Much better." Which is the honest truth.

"While you were being lazy, Germany capitulated." He leans in closer. "It was either the Americans or getting you into Berlin, towards the Soviets."

"I'm not complaining." I'm not convinced the Russians would have operated on me and looked after me while I got well enough to be awake. Considering the chaos and disarray on our own side, I'm not convinced *our* side would have looked after me.

Baldur reaches out to touch my shoulder. "There was no other way."

Maybe he has to repeat this to soothe his ruffled honour; he's not used to giving up, and he wouldn't have, if not for me. I do mean that much to him. I can't say I'm glad I was wounded, or that I welcome the current circumstances. The fact that he's sitting here is a miracle, that he's in one piece even more so. And how ironic that of the two of us, it would be me who was wounded in action—that danger would come for me, even though he kept racing into the heart of it. But then, poor Wischinsky's wife died before he did. Right from the outset, there's been no protection for civilians; we just didn't expect the war to devour our own country.

"I know," I say and take his hand with both of mine. I don't want to let him go. I don't want to see him race into the sky anymore to challenge death head-on. It's no longer necessary; the battle is lost, and we're both alive. "Are you going to stay?"

He glances at his guard, then back to me. "I'm not going anywhere. Not while you're still hurt. Not ever, if I can help it."

A gentle, warm, sweet pain spreads through my chest at those words. I want to pull him into an embrace, but we have to keep up appearances. Whatever we have can only be in secret, but I don't care as long as I know he is safe and sound.

GLOSSARY

Ami, Amis: Slang for American, Americans ("Yank," "Yanks")

Experte, Experten: Luftwaffe slang, "ace," "aces"

Geschwader: Wing

Gruppe: Group

Jagdgeschwader: Fighter wing

Katschmarek: Luftwaffe slang, "wingman"

Kneipe: Pub

Leutnant: Lieutenant

Luftwaffe: German Air Force

Rotte: Pair of two aircraft; consists of Rottenführer (pair leader) and Rottenflieger (pair flyer)

Schwarm: Literally "swarm." Group of four machines, part of a Staffel

Schwarzer Mann, Schwarze Männer: Literally "black man," "black men." Air force mechanics, called that because of their black coveralls

Staffel: Squadron (nine to twelve aircraft)

Staffelkameraden: Squadron comrades

Stuka: Short for Sturzkampfbomber, dive bomber

Wehrmacht: German Army

ALSO BY
ALEKSANDR VOINOV

Quid Pro Quo, with LA Witt
Take It Off, with LA Witt
If It Flies, with LA Witt
Incursion
Gold Digger
Country Mouse, with Amy Lane
City Mouse, with Amy Lane
Dark Soul Vols. 1–5
Break and Enter, with Rachel Haimowitz
Scorpion, Coming soon
Dark Edge of Honor, with Rhi Etzweiler
The Lion of Kent, with Kate Cotoner

For a full list, go to www.aleksandrvoinov.com/bookshelf.html

ABOUT THE
AUTHOR

Aleksandr Voinov is an emigrant German author living near London, where he is one of the unsung heroes in the financial services sector. His genres range from horror, science fiction, cyberpunk, and fantasy to contemporary, thriller, and historical erotic gay novels.

In his spare time, he goes weightlifting, explores historical sites, and meets other writers. He singlehandedly sustains three London bookstores with his ever-changing research projects. His current interests include special forces operations during World War II, pre-industrial warfare, European magical traditions, and how to destroy the world and plunge it into a nuclear winter without having the benefit of nuclear weapons.

Visit Aleksandr's website at www.aleksandrvoinov.com, his blog at www.aleksandrvoinov.blogspot.com, and follow him on Twitter, where he tweets as @aleksandrvoinov.

ACKNOWLEDGMENTS

Many thanks go to my editors, JoSelle and Rachel, who kept chiselling away and demanded I be more specific and thus kept driving me back to my research and reference material. Thanks also to my first readers: Peter, Anja, Aija, Sue (who tipped me off that the attacking planes in the raid on the airfield would likely be Mustangs), Heidi and Sara; my Brit-checkers, Alyssa and Alex Muir; and my final proofer, Alex Whitehall.

Luftwaffe history is a somewhat complex field, and even though I've probably seen all readily-available contemporary footage of German fighter operations and airfields (much to the chagrin of my partner, who was interested at first and grew more jaded with every DVD delivery featuring the history of the Luftwaffe and WWII fighter planes), I will inevitably have made mistakes.

Where possible, I've drawn on memoirs of German aces, especially Hermann Buchner, who relates the striking anecdote of Baron Wolfram von Richthofen and the "black men" in his memoir, *Stormbird*. I also used a number of Osprey Publishing titles for visual reference and to get an idea of the processes and flying characteristics of the planes I mention. I must have spent hours looking at the very fine illustrations, especially the Bf 109 cockpit layout. Readers will be grateful that none of that made it into the story. YouTube was helpful for referencing the sound of the historic planes and their movement, thanks to amateurs filming air shows.

Baldur's hometown is modelled on Templin, which I've visited, but the timing of the attack on Templin on March 6, 1944, didn't suit the story, so I changed it to a generic, very common name meaning simply "new city."

Despite my best attempts to get the research water-tight, I will have made mistakes, and these, as always, remain entirely mine.

Enjoy this book?
Find more historical fiction at
RiptidePublishing.com!

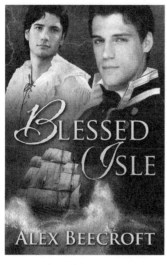

www.riptidepublishing.com/titles/
blessed-isle

www.riptidepublishing.com/titles/
collections/warriors-rome

Earn Bonus Bucks!

Earn 1 Bonus Buck for each dollar you spend. Find out how at
RiptidePublishing.com/news/bonus-bucks.

Win Free Ebooks for a Year!

Pre-order coming soon titles directly through our site and you'll
receive one entry into a drawing to win free books for a year!
Get the details at RiptidePublishing.com/contests.